HAPPY
HOPPY RABBIT

BY JUNE WOODMAN
ILLUSTRATED BY PAMELA STOREY

BRIMAX BOOKS · NEWMARKET · ENGLAND

It is Hoppy Rabbit's birthday.
He puts out all the things
for his birthday party.
He finds a cloth to put
on the table. He puts the
food on the table too. There
are lots of good things
to eat.

All Hoppy's friends come to the party. Paddy Dog and Bossy Bear come first.
"Happy Birthday, Hoppy!" they say.
"Here is a present for you," says Paddy. He gives Hoppy a big red ball.
"Thank you," says Hoppy, "I like to play games with a ball."

Bossy Bear has a present for Hoppy too.
"Oh, look. It is a kite!" says Hoppy.
"Look, here come Merry Mole and Flippy Frog," says Bossy. "Happy Birthday, Hoppy," they say. Flippy gives Hoppy a big bunch of flowers.
"I like flowers," says Hoppy.

Merry Mole has some carrots
for Hoppy.
"I like eating carrots,"
he says. "Thank you."
Then Cuddly Cat comes with
a big basket.
"Thank you," says Hoppy.
He puts all his presents
into the basket.

Here comes Dilly Duck with her three little ducklings. She has made a birthday cake for Hoppy.
The ducklings give him lots and lots of big balloons. Hoppy is very happy with all his birthday presents.

"Time to eat!" says Hoppy.
They all go to the table
and they begin to eat.
They eat and they eat until
all the food is gone.
"I like birthdays," says
Hoppy. "Time to play some
games now."

They go outside to play with the big red ball. Hoppy throws it to Paddy. He throws it high into the air. The others try to catch it. They jump up high, but no one can get the ball. Then Cuddly Cat jumps up on to the fence. Now she can catch it.

"This is a very good game!" says Cuddly.

The wind begins to blow.
"Good!" says Hoppy. "Now
I can play with my kite."
He gets the red and blue kite
and he begins to run. The
wind is blowing hard, and
the kite goes up in the air.
"Look at it fly!" says
Bossy Bear.

"Let me have a go," says Paddy.
The kite goes up in the air.
"Let me have a go," says Dilly.
She begins to run, but she does not see Flippy Frog.
BUMP!
She falls over poor Flippy.
Silly Dilly Duck!

Dilly lets go of the kite and it goes up into the air. "Oh no!" they all say. Hoppy, Paddy and Bossy jump up to catch it. But it is stuck high up in the tree. They cannot get it.

Poor Hoppy Rabbit.
He is not very happy now.
"Look!" says Bossy. "I can
get it for you."
Bossy gets up into the tree.
He gets the kite and he begins
to come down.

Then Bossy stops.
"Oh no!" he says.
"I am stuck!"
Bossy cannot get down.
"What can we do?" says Dilly.
"Look!" says Hoppy. He runs
to get all the balloons.
Then he gets the basket.
He ties the balloons to the
basket. Then he lets it go.

Up goes the basket!
It goes up into the tree.
"Get in, Bossy!" says Hoppy.
So Bossy gets into the basket
and it begins to come down.
Down and down it comes.
BUMP!
The basket is down,
Bossy is down,
and the kite is down too!
"What a happy birthday!"
says happy Hoppy Rabbit.

Say these words again

cloth	outside
friends	air
food	throws
eat	catch
first	jumps
present	wind
games	stuck